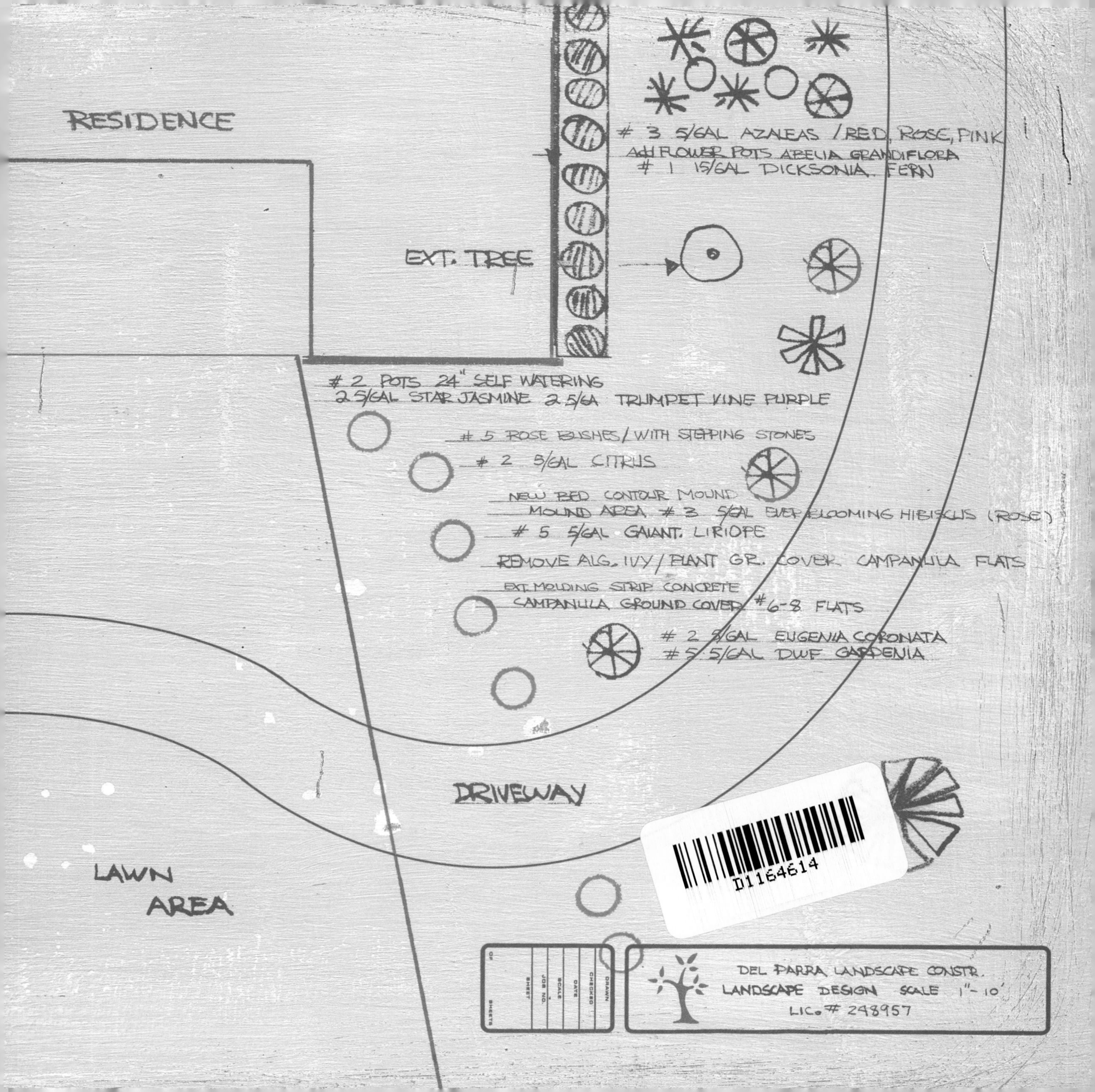
RESIDENCE
EXT. TREE
3 5/GAL AZALEAS / RED, ROSE, PINK
Add FLOWER POTS ABELIA GRANDIFLORA
1 15/GAL DICKSONIA FERN
2 POTS 24" SELF WATERING
2 5/GAL STAR JASMINE 2 5/GA TRUMPET VINE PURPLE
5 ROSE BUSHES / WITH STEPPING STONES
2 5/GAL CITRUS
NEW BED CONTOUR MOUND
MOUND AREA # 3 5/GAL EVER BLOOMING HIBISCUS (ROSE)
5 5/GAL GAIANT LIRIOPE
REMOVE ALG. IVY / PLANT GR. COVER CAMPANULA FLATS
EXT. MOLDING STRIP CONCRETE
CAMPANULA GROUND COVER #6-8 FLATS
2 5/GAL EUGENIA CORONATA
5 5/GAL DWF GARDENIA
DRIVEWAY
LAWN
AREA
D1164614
DEL PARRA LANDSCAPE CONSTR.
LANDSCAPE DESIGN SCALE 1"-10'
LIC. # 248957

Growing an Artist

To my family, who guides me in this wonderful chaotic journey called artist.
And to all those who work with their hands, head, and heart to make a better world.

SIMON & SCHUSTER BOOKS FOR YOUNG READERS
An imprint of Simon & Schuster Children's Publishing Division
1230 Avenue of the Americas, New York, New York 10020

The text for this book was set in Caecilia LT Std. • The illustrations for this book were rendered in acrylic paints on illustration board.
Manufactured in China • 0122 SCP • First Edition
2 4 6 8 10 9 7 5 3 1
Library of Congress Cataloging-in-Publication Data
Names: Parra, John, author, illustrator.
Title: Growing an artist : the story of a landscaper and his son / John Parra.
Description: First edition. | New York : A Paula Wiseman Book, Simon & Schuster Books for Young Readers, 2022. | Audience: Ages 4–8. | Audience: Grades 2–3. |
Summary: Today Juanito is accompanying his father who is in the landscaping business, and he takes his sketchbook along to draw anything that catches his eye, and gets to help his father plan an entire garden—and then help plant it. Includes an autobiographical note.
Identifiers: LCCN 2021022493 (print) | LCCN 2021022494 (ebook) | ISBN 9781534469273 (hardcover) | ISBN 9781534469280 (ebook)
Subjects: LCSH: Parra, John—Juvenile fiction. | Artists—Juvenile fiction. | Fathers and sons—Juvenile fiction. | Landscape gardening—Juvenile fiction. |
CYAC: Parra, John—Fiction. | Artists—Fiction. | Fathers and sons—Fiction. | Landscape gardening—Fiction. | Gardening—Fiction. | Mexican Americans—Fiction. |
LCGFT: Autobiographical fiction.
Classification: LCC PZ7.1.P3688 Gr 2022 (print) | LCC PZ7.1.P3688 (ebook) | DDC [E]—dc23
LC record available at https://lccn.loc.gov/2021022493
LC ebook record available at https://lccn.loc.gov/2021022494

GROWING AN ARTIST

THE STORY OF A LANDSCAPER AND HIS SON

JOHN PARRA

A Paula Wiseman Book
SIMON & SCHUSTER BOOKS FOR YOUNG READERS
New York London Toronto Sydney New Delhi

Landscape
Construction
Company

"Are you ready, mijo?" Papi asks. He smiles as I carry an armful of tools and supplies.

"Have a good day!" Mami calls.

Soon we rumble off into the cool morning air. Today is a BIG day. Today is the first time I get to help my papi at his work. He is a landscape contractor.

Our first stop is to pick up Javier. He has worked for my dad since I was small. Before that he lived in Mexico working on avocado farms. Javier asks if I remember the Spanish he taught me. "¿Cómo te llamas?" Javier asks.

"Me llamo Juanito," I reply.

"¿Listo para trabajar?" he says.

"Sí, listo," I answer.

He nods approvingly. "You are ready for work."

As we continue down the road, we sing loudly to the oldies radio station.

At Mrs. Tarbe's house, Javier shows me how to mow perfect lines in the grass, just like I've seen at baseball stadiums. Papi demonstrates how to shape and trim bushes.

When I look up, I see a face in the window next door. It's Alex from homeroom. He looks away and pretends not to see me. My heart sinks. We always say hi in school. I put my head down, feeling awkward, and continue to pick up leaves.

"Juanito!" Papi's soft call interrupts my thoughts of Alex. He pushes back the branches of a bougainvillea bush. I'm surprised to see a nest of baby birds chirping away. I grab my sketchbook and quickly draw.

Finally, with our electric blower, we clean all the sidewalks and drives. Sun shines through the clouds of dust.

At lunchtime I unwrap Mami's famous burrito: chorizo, avocado, and egg. I'm still thinking of Alex when I ask, "Papi, do you like your work?"

He pauses, then says, "You know, mijo, being your own boss is the best thing in the world. You have to work hard and sometimes you are treated like you are invisible, but when you do something you love and get to be creative, you feel proud." He notices my sketchbook and says, "Hey, you are getting so good." I smile.

The next stop is the nursery. Javier finds a store utility cart to drive to load up plants. There are bushes, trees, vines, and many flowers to choose from. I again pull out my sketchbook and begin to draw.

CARPINTERIA
NURSERY

With our purchases, we head to Mr. Sardisco's house. He is an old family friend who has more than two hundred rosebushes in his garden. When Papi shows him the special Busy Bee rosebush just for him, Mr. Sardisco is thrilled. "No one knows more about plants than your dad," he exclaims.

By now our truck is full of brush and waste.
"We need to head to the city dump," Papi announces.
"Fantastic," I say, "I love that place!"
Soon we pull up to the registration booth, then head up the winding road.

The dump will turn these branches and trimmings into mulch for planting. Papi unhitches the truck's clamps, lowers the tarp, and climbs back inside. I hear the hydraulics working hard. *Vroom, Vroom!* The back bed lifts up. We inch forward, and soon all the debris comes tumbling out. All three of us look at one another and shout: "¡Híjole!"

The final stop of the day is a house that looks much different from the ones we saw earlier. We ring the doorbell. Mr. and Mrs. Carroll are happy to see my dad. Together they discuss how to transform the overgrown yard into a special place. I look around and start to see its potential too.

That evening, I have an idea. “May I help with a landscape design?”

“Sí,” Papi agrees. “That would be fantastic!”

ARNOLDI'S CAFE

SKETCH
BOOK

Soon Papi and I are sitting at his worktable, drawing the lawn, flower beds, walkways, and trees.

I add colors to brighten the layout.

Hours pass and I become lost in the work. I forget to think about Alex.

"This is beautiful, mijo," Papi says.

The next day he comes home with a huge smile.

"The Carrolls love the design. We start breaking ground next week," he says.

"You have a gift," says Mami.

Landscape
Construction
Company

A few weeks later Papi, Javier, and I work to plant the last shrubs. The plans I helped to draw are about to be real.

I grab my sketchbook and turn the pages. I see the yards my dad has made beautiful. I see Javier hard at work. I remember Alex's face in the window. I turn to a blank page and begin to sketch. I will use my art to tell the stories of hardworking, passionate people who make the world more beautiful. I will tell their stories. I will tell my story.

Author's Note

The story of the little landscaper is the story of my childhood.

John Parra with his papi, Del

When I was growing up, I worked for my father, who ran his own landscape and construction company in Southern California. My father's parents had come from Chihuahua, Mexico, to El Paso, Texas, where my dad was born. When he was nine years old, his family moved to California's hot Central Valley. There, he labored throughout his youth (ages nine to about seventeen) alongside his siblings as a migrant farm worker. As he got older, he began working at a nursery in Bakersfield caring for plants. After serving in the United States Army he settled in Santa Barbara to begin learning the landscape business. It didn't take long for him to receive his contractor's license. Over time his business grew, and within a few years he became president of the regional tri-county chapter of the California Landscape Contractors Association.

Often my father's employees were migrants from Mexico who rented rooms in our own home and became part of our extended family. My parents encouraged them to take English classes, and many did. My father sponsored his laborers for citizenship. Eventually, a number of them went on to buy homes, begin families, and start successful businesses of their own.

I began accompanying my father to work when I was seven, at first helping with small tasks. By the time I was thirteen it was my part-time job. As a young artist, I loved to work on my father's landscape blueprints. For twelve years I learned from my father and even considered studying landscape architecture and design when I got older. Ultimately, I found my path studying illustration and fine art at the Art Center College of Design in Pasadena, California.

Landscape work was not easy. It was a physically demanding job done outdoors in all kinds of weather. I had to balance school, friends, life, art, and helping my dad. But working with him was rewarding. It was a creative outlet that nurtured my imagination, and my dad's eye for design and beauty inspired me as a young artist. It provided me with a strong work ethic and taught me responsibility and business. I am grateful for those days spent with my dad and proud that I could contribute to my family's business.

Mi familia

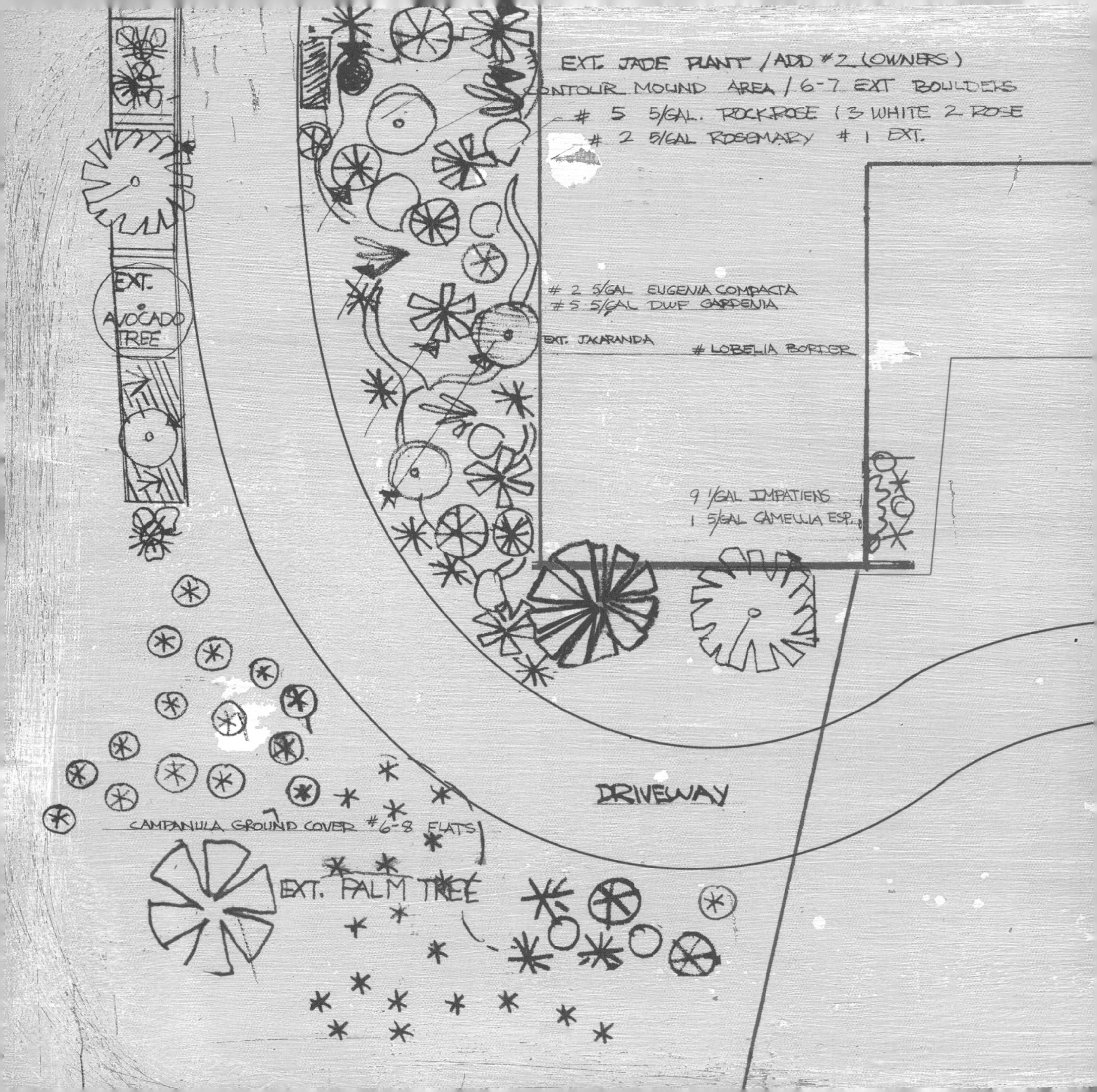

EXT. JADE PLANT / ADD #2 (OWNERS)
CONTOUR MOUND AREA / 6-7 EXT BOULDERS
5 5/GAL. ROCKROSE (3 WHITE 2 ROSE
2 5/GAL ROSEMARY # 1 EXT.
EXT. AVOCADO TREE
2 5/GAL EUGENIA COMPACTA
5 5/GAL DWF GARDENIA
EXT. JACARANDA
LOBELIA BORDER
9 1/GAL IMPATIENS
1 5/GAL CAMELLIA ESP.
DRIVEWAY
CAMPANULA GROUND COVER #6-8 FLATS
EXT. PALM TREE